Bear's Magic
and other stories

by CARLA STEVENS

Pictures by ROBERT J. LEE

SCHOLASTIC BOOK SERVICES

NEW YORK · TORONTO · LONDON · AUCKLAND · SYDNEY

Text copyright © 1976 by Carla Stevens. Illustrations copyright © 1976 by Scholastic Magazines, Inc. All rights reserved. Published by Scholastic Book Services, a division of Scholastic Magazines, Inc.

12 11 10 9 8 7 6 5 4 3 2   6 7 8 9/7 0 1/8

Printed in the U.S.A.

Contents

Wish I May, Wish I Might

Rabbit's lunch box
was very, very old.
Everyone in his class
had a lunch box
with pictures on it.
There were whales
on Woodchuck's lunch box.
And Possum had cars on his.

But Rabbit's lunch box
was just blue all over
and rusty in the corners.

Rabbit told his mother
how terrible his lunch tasted
in his blue lunch box.
No one
would sit next to him at school,
he said,
because his lunch box
was so old.

But his mother said
that he was lucky
to have such a fine old
lunch box.

One night,
Rabbit was waiting for supper
when he saw the first star
twinkling faintly in the sky.
He decided to make a wish.

"Star light, star bright,
First star I see tonight,
Wish I may, wish I might,
Have the wish I wish tonight."
Then he said,
"A new lunch box, please."

The next morning
when it was time
to leave for school,
his mother gave him
his same old lunch box.
Rabbit thought about the star.
It was very far away.
Probably his wish had not
reached the star yet.

That day at school
he sat next to Skunk,
and while he ate his lunch
he looked at the snakes
on Skunk's lunch box.

When school was over,
he went home
and put his lunch box
on the kitchen table.

Then he went outside
and sat down and waited.
The sun was setting in the west.
It was beginning to grow dark.
Soon the first evening star
twinkled in the sky.

"Star light, star bright,"
he called.
"First star I see tonight.
Wish I may, wish I might,
Have the wish I wish tonight."

This time he said in a loud voice,
"In case you didn't hear me
yesterday,
I would like a new lunch box,
please!"

But the next morning,
when he was ready to leave
for school,
his mother gave him
the same old lunch box.

Oh, well.
That star was certainly
far, far away.
His wish would probably take
a little while longer
to get there.

That day in school,
he sat next to Possum at lunch
and counted fourteen cars
on Possum's lunch box.

After baseball practice,
he hurried home
and put his lunch box
on the kitchen table.

Then he went outside
and looked up in the sky.
Soon the first evening star
appeared.
This time he stood and shouted.
  "Star light, star bright,
  First star I see tonight,
  Can you hear me?
  Wish I may, wish I might,
  Have the wish I wish tonight.
  As I said before,

  I WISH I COULD HAVE

  A NEW LUNCH BOX!"

Rabbit's mother
opened the kitchen door.
She gave Rabbit a funny look and
said it was time for supper.

The next morning
when Rabbit was ready to leave
for school,
his mother gave him
his same old lunch box.
He almost cried.

But he remembered what
his teacher told him. She said
that the evening star was
sixty-seven million miles away!
His wish would probably take
at least another day
to get there.

So he went to school
and ate his lunch
and studied the blue whale
and the white whale
and the sperm whale
on Woodchuck's lunch box.

Finally school was over
and Rabbit went home.

His mother was waiting for him
at the door.
Rabbit gave her
his old blue lunch box.
And his mother
gave him something back.

A brand new lunch box!

This lunch box had trucks on it —
a dump truck,
a garbage truck,
a tow truck —
more than ten different trucks!
Rabbit hugged
his new lunch box.
He hugged his mother.

Then he ran outside
and called in a very, very,
very loud voice,
"THANK YOU,
EVENING STAR!"

The Birthday Party Wish

Not very long ago,
there lived a mouse
who loved birthdays more than
anything else in the world.
When she was six years old,
her parents gave her
a birthday party.
All her friends came.

First, they played games.
They played
Pin the Tail on the Bunny
and Hide the Button.

Then it was time
to have cake and ice cream.
Before she blew out the candles
on her beautiful chocolate cake,
she made a wish.

"I wish I could have a birthday
every day,"
she said to herself.
Whoosh!
She blew out all the candles.

After everyone had cake
and ice cream,
Mouse opened her presents.
She got a ball, a jump rope,
crayons, checkers,
and pick-up-sticks.

At last everyone went home.
Mouse was tired
from all the excitement.

She went to bed early
and fell sound asleep.

Well, the next day
at three o'clock
(which is the time
for birthday parties)
there was a loud knock
on the door.
Mouse opened it.

All her friends
came piling into her house.
"Happy birthday!" they shouted.
She was surprised.
It was my birthday yesterday,
she thought.
But she didn't say that out loud.
First they played games.
Then it was time for cake
and ice cream.

Mouse was having fun.
So she made the same wish
on her chocolate cake that
she made the day before.

Whoosh!
She blew out all the candles.
Then she opened her presents.
She was a little surprised to see
they were the same presents
that she got yesterday.
Now she had two of everything,
but she didn't care.

Finally everyone went home.

When she went to bed that night,
she was very excited.

Maybe, tomorrow, she would have
another party!

The next day, at three o'clock,
all her friends
came piling into her house again.
They brought her presents
and they played.

They had cake and ice cream
and Mouse made the same wish
when she blew out her candles.
She knew then
that she would have
another birthday
the next day,
and the next,
and the next.

But on the day after that,
she began to get tired of those
same presents.

She had six jump ropes,
six games of checkers,
six boxes of crayons,
six bunches of pick-up-sticks,
and six balls.

She was even more tired of
chocolate cake.

So when it came time
to blow out the candles,
she changed her wish.

She said to herself,
"I wish my birthday
would be over today."
She took a deep breath
and blew. *Whoosh!*
All the candles went out —
except one.

Oh dear!

The next day she had another
birthday.
When it came time
to make her wish,
she wished even harder
that her birthday would be over.
Then she blew with all her might.

And guess what!
All the candles went out,
and that was the end
of Mouse's birthday
for another year!

At her seven-year-old
birthday party,
she made
a much more sensible wish.
"I wish I could have pancakes
for breakfast tomorrow morning."

And she did!

Bear's Magic

It all started on Friday
when Bear wished it would snow.
He got new snowshoes for Christmas,
and he wanted to use them.

So he said out loud to himself,
"I wish it would snow."

Very soon, tiny flakes of snow
began to drift slowly down out of the sky.
It snowed all night.

The next morning,
Bear looked out of the window.

What a surprise!
He must have some powerful magic
to make it snow like that.
There was plenty of snow for snowshoeing.
So he said out loud,
"I wish it would stop snowing!"
And later that day it did.

Bear had fun snowshoeing all day Sunday.
He wanted to snowshoe on Monday, too.
But his father said
that he had to go to school.

Just before school was over that day,
his teacher told the class
that they were going to have
an arithmetic test tomorrow.

"Ah ha!" Bear thought.
"I will fool her!
I will wish that there is no school
tomorrow."

On his way home, he made the wish.
That night he didn't study for his test.
He just played with his toys.

When he woke up the next morning,
his mother was standing beside his bed.
She said he didn't have to get up so early.
It was too slippery outside
to go to school.

"I knew it! I knew it!" said Bear.

"You knew what?" asked his mother.

"Oh, nothing," Bear said.

He lay in bed for a while,
thinking that he must be the most magic bear
in the whole world.
Then he got up
and played all day with his toys.

The next morning there was school again.
The first thing his teacher did
was to pass out the arithmetic test.

"Oh help!" said Bear to himself.
"I'd better use my magic."
So he said out loud,
"I wish to get 100 on my test."

"No talking, Bear," his teacher said.

Bear looked at the test.
There were quite a few examples
he did not know how to do.

He wasn't too worried, though.

Soon his magic would begin to work.

But no answers came into his head.

"Come on, magic!" he said.
"Get going!"

But nothing happened.

His teacher walked by his desk.
She looked at Bear's paper.
"Bear, please stay after school today.
You need extra help."

So Bear stayed after school
and got extra help
while everyone else went sliding
on the icy hillside near his house.

On his way home,
Bear thought about his magic.
Suddenly he knew what was wrong.

His magic would not work *in* school.
It would only work *out* of school!

He decided to make another wish —
an easy wish,
just to get his magic working again.
He said out loud,
"I wish I could have spaghetti
for supper tonight."

It was late when he got home.
His father said to wash his paws
because supper was almost ready.

Bear washed his paws.
Then he sat down at the table.
He was so hungry,
he could hardly wait to eat his spaghetti.

Soon his father came in from the kitchen
with a big plate.
He put it in front of Bear.
Bear looked.

Oh help!
There on his plate
was not spaghetti at all, but
liver!

How could his magic give him **liver** instead of spaghetti?

If his magic was going to get *that* mixed up,
he'd better not take any more chances.
No more wishes for him!
After supper he went to his room
and did all his homework.

And the next day,
he didn't have to stay
after school for extra help
because he got 100
on his spelling test!